DATE DUE

M. G.	G	MAY 0	M
APR 15	RV	APR 29	
SEP 10	H	MAY 13	LT
DEC 20			
FEB 04			
OCT 27	AK		
APR 07			
NOV 81			
APR 3			
APR 12			
APR 28	LK		
APR 30	P. S		
DEC 7			

GAYLORD   PRINTED IN U.S.A.

THE
EASTER BUNNY
THAT OVERSLEPT

Library of Congress Cataloging in Publication Data
Friedrich, Priscilla. The Easter bunny that overslept.
Summary: Having slept past Easter, the Easter bunny tries to distribute his eggs on Mother's Day, the Fourth of July, and Halloween, but no one is interested. At Christmas time it is Santa who gets him back on track. [1. Tardiness—Fiction. 2. Easter—Fiction. 3. Christmas—Fiction] I. Friedrich, Otto, (date). II. Adams, Adrienne, ill. III. Title.
PZ7.F9152Eas 1983   [E] 82-13013 ISBN 0-688-01540-9
ISBN 0-688-01541-7 (lib. bdg.)

For Liesel, Molly, Nicholas, and Amelia

by Priscilla and Otto Friedrich
illustrated by Adrienne Adams

THE
EASTER BUNNY
THAT OVERSLEPT

Lothrop, Lee & Shepard Books   New York

In his cozy warm burrow under the ground, the Easter Bunny was sound asleep. He was dreaming of Easter and the brightly painted eggs that he was going to bring to all the children. Easter came at last, but the Easter Bunny kept right on sleeping. There was no sun to wake him up, and it rained all day long. The children were very disappointed not to find eggs hidden on their lawns or in their homes. But their parents had bought some jelly beans, so they weren't completely forgotten. It rained every day for a month—and the Easter Bunny slept right on!

Early in May the rain stopped. The sun shone into the Easter Bunny's burrow and woke him up. He yawned and stretched, and put on his new clothes, because, of course, he thought it was Easter time. He even sang a little song to himself—

I hip and I hop
My eggs are blue
Red, and green, too
A pink one for you
All nice and new
Hippety-hop!

Soon he came to a pink house where a mother and a father, a girl and a boy, and a baby were sitting under an apple tree.

They were eating chocolates—all except the baby. He was too little for chocolates, so he held a cracker.

The Easter Bunny hopped up and started singing Happy Easter to You. It had the same tune as Happy Birthday.

When the Easter Bunny finished his song, he offered his basket of Easter eggs.

"What's all this?" asked the father. "What is this rabbit doing here?"

"Why, it's the Easter Bunny," said the little girl.

"But Easter was weeks ago!" said the mother. "Today is *Mother's Day.*"

"Bye-Bye!" said the baby. These were the only words he could say, so he said them over and over. The Easter Bunny decided to try somewhere else. He looked back sadly, as he hopped to a yellow house nearby. But no one there wanted any Easter eggs either. He hopped all through the neighborhood, but everywhere he heard the same thing. It was too late for Easter eggs. Some of the people even scolded him for not being on time.

The Easter Bunny went back to his burrow. He looked at his beautiful basket of Easter eggs that nobody wanted. He thought and he thought. Finally he had an idea.

"I'll be a Fourth-of-July Bunny!" he said to himself. And he started re-painting his eggs red, white and blue. Then he made himself a red, white and blue hat. And on the Fourth of July, he started out again.

It was a very hot day, and the bunny's basket began to feel heavier and heavier as he hopped along. When he came to the center of the town, he saw a crowd of people watching a parade.

The band came first, with trumpets and trombones going "Ooom-pah-pah." Then came soldiers, then came the Boy Scouts and the Girl Scouts carrying flags.

And with them, proudly carrying his basket full of red, white and blue eggs, hopped the Fourth-of-July Bunny.

"Stop the parade!" shouted an officer. "Stop! Halt!"

Everyone stopped.

"What's all this?" the officer demanded. "Who are you?"

"Well, I'm really the Easter Bunny," the rabbit said in a very small voice. He was beginning to be a bit frightened. "But I overslept a little and started out too late and nobody wanted my Easter eggs. So I thought I'd be a Fourth-of-July Bunny."

"The Fourth-of-July is no time for *eggs!*" The officer looked very cross. "Now go away!"

Just then a great firecracker went

BOOM!

The children all clapped their hands in delight at the noise. None of them paid any attention to the Easter Bunny.

Bang! Bang! Bang! Smaller firecrackers were going off now. Then a cluster of great rockets went zooming into the sky and turned into a cluster of stars.

The parade marched on, and the Easter Bunny was left alone.

He tried knocking at several more doors, but everyone thought he was joking. So he went back to his burrow and fell asleep again. The summer passed and the days grew shorter. The leaves blew down from the trees, and still the Easter Bunny slept.

One black night when the wind howled outside, the Easter Bunny heard a loud knock. He jumped up and opened his door. Three little white ghosts stood in front of him.

"BOO!"

Just then the wind blew very hard. The white sheets flapped on the three little ghosts. The Easter Bunny looked down and saw three pairs of brown shoes.

It was Halloween.

"A trick or a treat!" one of the ghosts cried.

"Wait right there," the Easter Bunny said happily, and he went back into his den to get his Easter eggs.

"A trick or a treat!" the children repeated as he returned with his basket. When they saw the red, white and blue eggs, the tallest child said, "What is this?"

"They're Fourth-of-July eggs," said the Easter Bunny.

"But this is Halloween!" said the middle-sized child.

"Well, they're really Easter eggs," the unhappy bunny explained. But he was too tired to tell his whole story all over again because he already knew that nobody wanted his eggs.

"Easter eggs on Halloween," the smallest child said. "That's no treat."

The Easter Bunny hung his head. He looked so sad that the children didn't even play a trick on him. They just ran away laughing.

"Easter eggs on Halloween!" they shouted, their voices getting farther and farther away. "Easter eggs on Halloween! Whoever heard of such a thing!"

The Easter Bunny stood in his doorway and watched them go. He began to shiver. The wind was cold and blowing harder. He

waited and waited for some more children to come. It started to
snow. Suddenly, a fierce gale swept the little rabbit off his feet and
carried him high up in the air.

When at last he came down, he blinked and rubbed his eyes. At first all he could see was snow. Then he caught sight of a sign that said

SANTA'S HOUSE

The sign was shaped like an arrow and it was pointing to a curving path that led between two rows of Christmas trees.

The Easter Bunny hopped down the path and there, just around the bend, he saw the house. The next moment he was knocking timidly on the door.

Santa himself opened it. "Well, bless my soul!" he said, when he saw the bunny on his doorstep. "Come in! Come in!"

So the Easter Bunny went in, and once more he told his story—how he had overslept, how nobody wanted his eggs, how he tried to be a Fourth-of-July Bunny, how he had been chased away, how the children had come to his burrow to frighten him on Halloween.

"Well, well," said Santa Claus. "Well, well, well! There's nothing we can do about your Easter eggs, of course. But if you want to help make the children happy, I have plenty of work for you to do."

And almost before he knew it, the Easter Bunny was busy painting toy fire engines, and tops, and doll beds and many more toys.

He was having such a good time, he forgot all about the Easter eggs that nobody wanted.

On Christmas Eve, Santa loaded the toys on his reindeer sleigh, and when he was ready to start, he said to the bunny, "That's the biggest load I ever had. Maybe you'd better come along and help me tonight."

So the Easter Bunny hopped in the sleigh next to Santa and off they flew through the sky.

Sometimes Santa would say the chimney was a little too narrow for him to climb down.

Then the Easter Bunny would take some toys from Santa's pack, slide easily down the narrow chimney, and put the toys in the children's stockings that were hanging by the fireplace.

And Santa Claus would say: "I never could go up and down all those chimneys as fast as that!"

And they would ride gaily on to the next house.

After they had delivered the last present they went back to Santa's house for cakes and hot chocolate. The Easter Bunny began to feel a little tired from all his traveling. He decided to go back to his burrow and sleep until Easter came again.

"Wait a minute," Santa Claus said. "I have a Christmas present for you, too." He reached deep into his sack and brought out a beautiful gold alarm clock.

"Oh, thank you, thank you, Santa Claus. I'll set it to go off Easter Sunday."

And the next year when the gold alarm clock began to ring, the Easter Bunny jumped up and filled *two* baskets full of eggs. Then he hopped up to the same pink house that he had visited the year before. A little boy called "Hi, Easter Bunny." It was the same baby who could only say "Bye-bye" the year before.

"Happy Easter!" the Easter Bunny called gaily. He offered the little boy an Easter egg, and the little boy took it.

The Easter Bunny was very happy. It was so nice to be right on time. And because of his gold alarm clock, he was never late delivering his Easter eggs again.